CH

ARTEMIS

Goddess of Hunting and Protector of Animals

BY TERI TEMPLE

ILLUSTRATED BY ROBERT SQUIER

The Child's World

Published by The Child's World®
1980 Lookout Drive • Mankato, MN 56003-1705
800-599-READ • www.childsworld.com

Acknowledgments
The Child's World®: Mary Berendes, Publishing Director
The Design Lab: Design and production
Red Line Editorial: Editorial direction

Design elements: Maksym Dragunov/Dreamstime;
Dreamstime

Photographs © Shutterstock Images, 5, 18; Bigstock, 12;
Bettmann/Corbis/AP Images, 14; Georgios Kollidas/
Shutterstock Images, 16; Giovanni Benintende/
Shutterstock, 20; Giulio Romano, 24; Bill McKelvie/
Shutterstock Images, 28

ISBN 9781614732563
LCCN 2012932432

Printed in the United States of America
Mankato, MN
December 2012
PA02157

CONTENTS

INTRODUCTION, 4

CHARACTERS AND PLACES, 6

THE GODDESS OF THE HUNT, 8

PRINCIPAL GODS OF GREEK MYTHOLOGY—
A FAMILY TREE, 30

THE ROMAN GODS, 31

FURTHER INFORMATION, 32

INDEX, 32

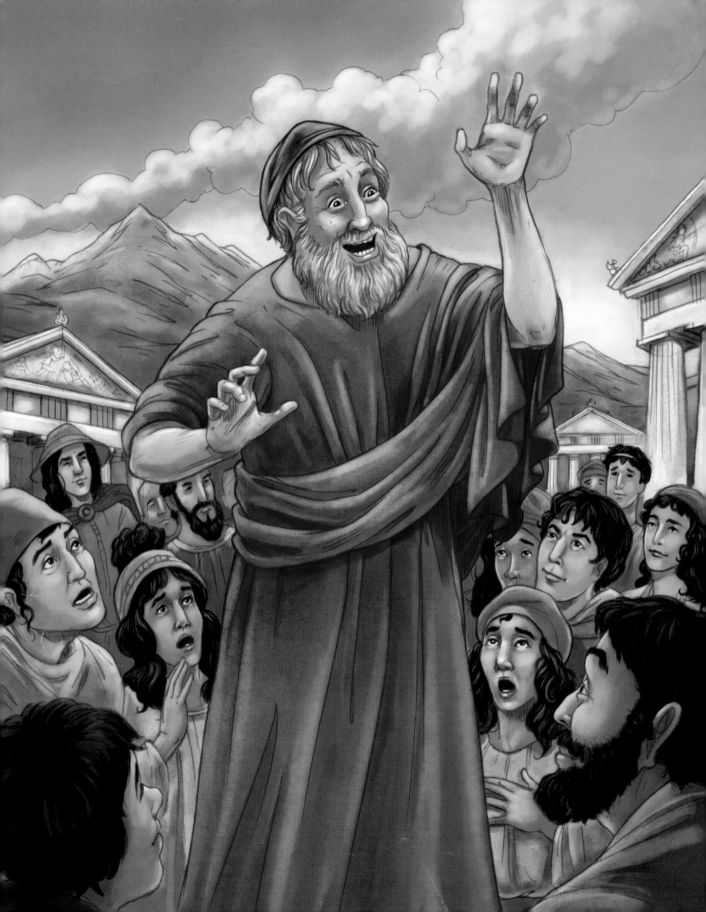

INTRODUCTION

Long ago in ancient Greece and Rome, most people believed that gods and goddesses ruled their world. Storytellers shared the adventures of these gods to help explain all the mysteries in life. The gods were immortal, meaning they lived forever. Their stories were full of love and tragedy, fearsome monsters, brave heroes, and struggles for power. The storytellers wove aspects of Greek customs and beliefs into the tales. Some stories told of the creation of the world and the origins of the gods. Others helped explain natural events such as earthquakes and storms. People believed the tales, which over time became myths.

The ancient Greeks and Romans worshiped the gods by building temples and statues in their honor. They felt the gods would protect and guide them. People passed down the myths through the generations by word of mouth. Later, famous poets such as Homer and Hesiod wrote them down. Today, these myths give us a unique look at what life was like in ancient Greece more than 2,000 years ago.

ANCIENT GREEK SOCIETIES

IN ANCIENT GREECE, CITIES, TOWNS, AND THEIR SURROUNDING FARMLANDS WERE CALLED CITY-STATES. THESE CITY-STATES EACH HAD THEIR OWN GOVERNMENTS. THEY MADE THEIR OWN LAWS. THE INDIVIDUAL CITY-STATES WERE VERY INDEPENDENT. THEY NEVER JOINED TO BECOME ONE WHOLE NATION. THEY DID, HOWEVER, SHARE A COMMON LANGUAGE, RELIGION, AND CULTURE.

MOUNT OLYMPUS
The mountaintop home of the 12 Olympic gods

Aegean Sea

MOUNT SIPYLUS
The mountain that Niobe fled to after her children were buried

DELOS, GREECE
An island in Greece where Leto gave birth to Apollo and Artemis

ANCIENT GREECE

CRETE

ACTAEON (ak-TEE-uhn)
Hunter who Artemis transformed into a stag

AGAMEMNON (ag-uh-MEM-nahn)
Leader of the Greek forces in the Trojan War

ALOADAE (al-oh-EY-dee)
Twin giants Otus and Ephialtes; sons of Poseidon

APOLLO (a-POL-lo)
God of sun, music, healing, and prophecy; son of Zeus and Leto; twin to Artemis

OLYMPIAN GODS
Demeter, Hermes, Hephaestus, Aphrodite, Ares, Hera, Zeus, Poseidon, Athena, Apollo, Artemis, and Dionysus

TROJAN WAR
War between the ancient Greeks and Trojans

ARTEMIS (AHR-tuh-mis)
Goddess of the hunt and the moon; daughter of Zeus and Leto; twin to Apollo

CALLISTO (kuh-LIS-toh)
Nymph companion of Artemis

CYCLOPES (SIGH-clopes)
One-eyed giants; children of Gaea and Uranus

EILEITHYIA (EHL-ih-thee-ah)
Goddess of childbirth; daughter of Zeus and Hera

HERA (HEER-uh)
Queen of the gods; married to Zeus

HERMES (HUR-meez)
Messenger to the gods; god of travel and trade; Son of Zeus

LETO (LEE-toh)
Titan goddess; wife of Zeus; mother of Apollo and Artemis

MELEAGER (mel-ee-AY-jur)
Greek hero who killed the Calydonian Boar

ORION (oh-RY-uhn)
A handsome giant killed by Artemis; son of Poseidon

PAN (PAN)
God of nature; son of Hermes; has the legs, horns, and tail of a goat

POSEIDON (puh-SY-duhn)
God of the sea and earthquakes; brother to Zeus

ZEUS (ZOOS)
Supreme ruler of the heavens and weather and of the gods who lived on Mount Olympus; youngest son of Cronus and Rhea; married to Hera; father of many gods and heroes

High atop Mount Olympus was the magnificent home of the Olympic gods and goddesses. They ruled over the heavens and protected Earth. Zeus was their supreme ruler. His wife was the lovely goddess Hera.

Everything on Olympus should have been perfect. It was far from it. Zeus believed he needed more wives so he could have many more children. All of his children would be given some of his power. They would become heroes, rulers, and even gods themselves. But Hera was a jealous wife. She did not like sharing Zeus.

Zeus was afraid of Hera's wrath. He often snuck behind her back to see other maidens. One was the beautiful goddess Leto. When Hera discovered Zeus had married Leto, she was fuming. Then Hera found out that Leto was expecting twins. Her rage exploded.

Hera set a plan for revenge in motion. She ordered all of the lands in the world to refuse Leto shelter. Hera also sent her serpent Python to torment Leto. With no place to rest, Leto was chased from place to place. She thought she would never find a safe place to give birth to her twins.

There was still hope. Poseidon, the god of the sea, had just created a new island. It was floating on the water. He had not yet anchored it down. It was the island of Delos. There was nothing on the island but a single palm tree. In its shade, Leto could finally rest. But Hera's tricks were not over yet. She refused to let her daughter Eileithyia, the goddess of childbirth, attend to the births. Without her help, no child could be born.

The other goddesses on Mount Olympus felt sorry for Leto. They tried to convince Hera to change her mind. They offered her a beautiful necklace made of gold and amber. Hera could not resist. She allowed Eileithyia to travel to Delos. On the island, Leto finally gave birth to her babies.

First came Artemis. She was as lovely as the moon. Artemis would become the goddess of the hunt and protector of all newborn creatures. Then came her twin brother Apollo. He was as glorious as the sun, fair-haired and bright. Apollo would become the god of the sun, music, healing, and prophecy. A prophecy is a prediction of what is to come. Zeus was joyful at the births of his new son and daughter. He blessed the island. It became the richest of all islands in Greece.

As Artemis grew, she asked her father Zeus for many favors. First she asked for all the mountains in the world as her home. Artemis then asked for nymphs to be her attendants. She wanted companions, but did not wish to marry. Artemis preferred to spend her time hunting in the forests and mountains.

She asked Zeus for a bow and arrows like her brothers. He honored all of her requests. Zeus asked the Cyclopes to create a special silver bow and arrows. The arrows would give her prey a swift and painless death. Artemis then received her adored hunting dogs from the god Pan. Some were black-and-white spotted and some were red. The hounds were faster than the wind and as fierce as lions. In a catch worthy of a goddess, Artemis captured four deer during a hunt. The deer were large as bulls with antlers of gold. They pulled Artemis through the woods in a golden chariot.

PAN: GOD OF THE WOODS

PAN WAS THE WILD AND UNRULY SON OF THE GOD HERMES. HE WAS HALF-MAN AND HALF-GOAT. ANCIENT GREEKS BELIEVED HE HAD THE POWER TO FILL HUMANS WITH EXTREME TERROR.

THE WORD *PANIC* IS DERIVED FROM HIS NAME. PAN WAS THE GOD OF WOODS AND PASTURES. HE WAS KNOWN FOR HIS ABILITY TO PLAY BEAUTIFUL MUSIC ON THE PANPIPES. PAN WOULD BECOME ONE OF THE MOST POPULAR GODS OF GREEK MYTHOLOGY.

OVID

OVID WAS A GREAT ROMAN POET. HE WAS BORN
IN SULMONA, ITALY, IN 43 BC. OVID IS BEST
KNOWN FOR HIS CLEVER POEMS ABOUT LOVE.

Artemis and Apollo remained close siblings and friends. They were both excellent at archery and enjoyed hunting together. Apollo and Artemis were fiercely loyal to their mother Leto. They did not take insult of her lightly. Revenge by the gods was often swift and harsh. One tragic character to feel their wrath was Niobe, queen of Thebes. Niobe had 14 children—seven sons and seven daughters. During a ceremony to honor Leto, Niobe foolishly bragged about the number of children she had. She mocked Leto for only having two children. When Leto learned of this, she sent Apollo and Artemis to seek revenge. She asked them to kill all of Niobe's children.

Apollo killed the seven sons as they practiced their athletics. Artemis killed all seven daughters with her deadly bow and arrows. Niobe's children lay unburied for nine days because Zeus had turned all of Thebes to stone. On the tenth day the gods had pity. They allowed Niobe's sons and daughters to be buried. In shock and grief she fled to Mount Sipylus. Once there, Niobe turned to stone. Endless tears flowed from the rock. She symbolized eternal sadness to the ancient Greeks.

OVID'S GREATEST WORK WAS THE EPIC POEM CALLED *METAMORPHOSES*. THE POEM TELLS MORE THAN 200 TALES FROM GREEK AND ROMAN MYTHS. THE TRAGEDY OF NIOBE IS JUST ONE OF THEM.

Artemis required her attendants to follow a life of purity like herself. Artemis could be cruel to those who upset her. The nymph Callisto learned this the hard way. Zeus had fallen in love with Callisto. She was a favorite companion of Artemis. Artemis was furious when she discovered Callisto was pregnant. The goddess turned Callisto into a bear. Years later, Callisto's son killed her, not knowing that the bear was his mother.

Another sad tale involved the nymph Echo. She fell in love with a beautiful youth named Narcissus. He rejected her. As punishment for his cruelty, Artemis caused him to fall in love with his own reflection. Day after day he gazed at the face he saw in the pond. Echo kept him company, always hoping for his love. The ancient Greeks believed she faded away until all that remained was her voice. Narcissus also wasted away and died. All that remained was a white flower, which bears his name.

NYMPHS

NYMPHS WERE PART OF A CLASS OF LESSER GODS IN GREEK MYTHOLOGY. THEY WERE PICTURED AS GRACEFUL AND BEAUTIFUL MAIDENS. NYMPHS LIVED IN AND WATCHED OVER THE SEAS, RIVERS, WOODS, TREES, MOUNTAINS, AND MEADOWS. EACH TYPE OF NYMPH HAD A SPECIAL NAME. THEY WERE OFTEN THE ATTENDANTS OF THE OLYMPIC GODS AND GODDESSES AND HAD VERY LONG LIVES.

Sometimes Artemis dealt out punishment to those who meant her no harm. Actaeon was one such unlucky fellow. He was well known as a hunter of great skill. He spent his days in the forest with his hunting hounds and traveling companions.

Actaeon wandered away from his hunting party one day. Walking alone, he came upon a clearing in the woods. In surprise, he realized what he saw was the goddess Artemis. She was bathing in a large pool surrounded by her nymph attendants. Actaeon stumbled away in shock. Artemis was furious that a mere human had seen her naked. In anger, she turned Actaeon into a stag.

GREEK THEATER

THE ANCIENT GREEKS INVENTED THEATER. THE VERY FIRST ORGANIZED THEATER PRODUCTION TOOK PLACE IN ATHENS IN 534 BC. THE THEATERS WERE STRUCTURES SHAPED LIKE HALF-CIRCLES. THEY WERE BUILT INTO HILLSIDES. THAT WAY THE SEATS COULD BE SET ONE ABOVE THE OTHER AROUND THE STAGE. THE STORY OF ACTAEON WAS A FAVORITE TOPIC OF ANCIENT GREEK THEATER

Actaeon felt different. But it was not until he saw his reflection in a river that he knew what the goddess had done. He was no longer human. When Actaeon heard his hounds off in the distance he was relieved. Then Actaeon realized the hounds were hunting him. They did not know their master. Instead they chased him down and killed him.

Orion was another hunting companion of Artemis. He was a handsome and lively giant. He was also a talented hunter. There are many legends that surround Orion. They all involve his early death. In all of the tales, Artemis is responsible for killing Orion. Some say Orion met his sad fate after he bragged he would kill all of the wild animals on Earth. Artemis sent a scorpion after him to sting him to death. In another version, Artemis shot him with her arrows after he assaulted her.

The most common tale involves Artemis's brother Apollo. He was jealous of the friendship Orion and Artemis shared. One day the siblings were out hunting in Crete. Apollo saw Orion swimming far out at sea. Apollo saw a chance to rid himself of the giant. He challenged his sister to try and hit the distant object they could see in the water. Artemis was an excellent shot, so she accepted. She easily hit the target. She pierced Orion's temple with an arrow. When she realized she had killed her friend, Artemis placed him in the sky as a constellation.

SCORPIUS CONSTELLATION

THE SCORPIUS CONSTELLATION IS A GROUP OF STARS THAT LIES ALONG THE PATH OF EARTH'S ORBIT OF THE SUN.

THE WORD *SCORPIUS* IS LATIN FOR *SCORPION*. IT IS PART OF 12 CONSTELLATIONS THAT MAKE UP THE ZODIAC. SCORPIUS CAN BE FOUND IN THE SOUTHERN SKY BETWEEN LIBRA AND SAGITTARIUS. THE ANCIENT GREEKS BELIEVED IT WAS A SYMBOL OF THE SCORPION THAT STUNG AND KILLED ORION.

21

Orion was not the only giant Artemis had to deal with. She had trouble with the giants Otus and Ephialtes as well. They were the twin sons of Poseidon known as the Aloadae giants. Artemis first met them when they tried to take over Mount Olympus. They were very tall and strong, but they were no match for the gods. Apollo defeated Otus and Ephialtes during the attack.

Artemis met them again when they decided to look for wives. Their plan was to kidnap the goddesses Hera and Artemis. The twins then planned to marry the goddesses, by force if necessary. Ephialtes had chosen Hera, since she was the queen of all the gods. Otus preferred the purity of Artemis. Artemis and Hera knew they were not as strong as the giants. So they came up with a plan to trick them.

Artemis changed herself into a white deer while the brothers were not looking. She then darted between them. Distracted, Otus and Ephialtes did not see each other when they threw their spears. Artemis was so fast that their throws missed her completely. Instead, both giants died instantly when their spears pierced each other.

Artemis did not like to be ignored. Several kings from ancient Greece learned that this was a terrible mistake. King Oeneus of Calydon was busy ruling his kingdom. One season he forgot to offer the first fruits of their harvest to Artemis. Feeling slighted, Artemis decided to punish the king. She sent a monstrous boar to attack his lands and frighten the people. To get rid of the horrible beast, King Oeneus needed help.

A call went out to all the greatest heroes of Greece. The hunting party included some of the finest hunters of all time. They included Jason, Theseus, Meleager, and Atalanta. The hunt to take the boar was bloody and fierce. Several men were killed. Atalanta was the only woman in the group. She was the first to wound the boar. Meleager was in love with Atalanta. So when he finally killed the boar, Meleager awarded Atalanta its hide. Calydon was once again safe, for now.

ATALANTA

Atalanta was well known in Greek mythology as a gifted hunter. She was left by her parents at birth and raised by a female bear. She took part in the hunt for the Calydonian boar and is credited with the first hit. Atalanta and her husband Melanion were later turned into lions after they offended Zeus.

King Agamemnon may have paid the biggest price for insulting Artemis. As king of Mycenae, he was to lead the Greek forces in the coming war with Troy. He and his men decided to hunt while waiting for the winds to change. They needed good winds to set sail for Troy. During the hunt, Agamemnon expertly took down a stag. He then bragged to the hunting party that his shot was as good as one from the goddess Artemis.

It was no surprise that Artemis did not like his boast. On the eve of the Trojan War she stranded the fleet in Greece. A soothsayer was able to figure out the cause. A soothsayer is a person who could predict events. The soothsayer told Agamemnon how he could get back in good favor with the goddess. He would need to sacrifice his daughter Iphigenia. When he had done this, all of the fleet's problems would be removed.

Agamemnon tried to sacrifice his daughter. At the last minute however, Artemis placed a deer in Iphigenia's place on the altar. She then whisked Iphigenia off to the country of Tauris. There she became a priestess to honor Artemis. Agamemnon discovered that dealing with the gods could be very tricky.

The goddess Artemis had many good qualities. She was the protector of the young, both animals and humans. But the ancient Greeks linked Artemis with death as well. As the goddess of the hunt, she brought about a swift end with her arrows. They also believed she could use her arrows to punish people or to spread disease.

Artemis was sometimes known by different names. In Greece, she was often confused with Selene, the primary goddess of the moon. Artemis was also adopted into the Roman myths as Diana, their goddess of the moon.

Artemis was the center of many festivals. At some festivals children would wear bearskins and dance as bears. These dances were to recognize their maturing bodies. Young girls would offer up their youthful belongings to Artemis on the eve of their weddings. Hunters also made sacrifices for a successful hunt. The goddess Artemis plays an important role in the myths of ancient Greece.

TEMPLE OF ARTEMIS

THE TEMPLE OF ARTEMIS WAS BUILT AROUND 550 BC IN EPHESUS, AN ANCIENT CITY IN TURKEY. THE TEMPLE WAS FAMOUS FOR ITS ENORMOUS SIZE AND ITS ARTWORK. ONLY COPIES OF THE STATUE THAT WAS IN THE TEMPLE HAVE SURVIVED. THE TEMPLE WAS DESTROYED IN 262 AD.

PRINCIPAL GODS OF GREEK MYTHOLOGY – A FAMILY TREE

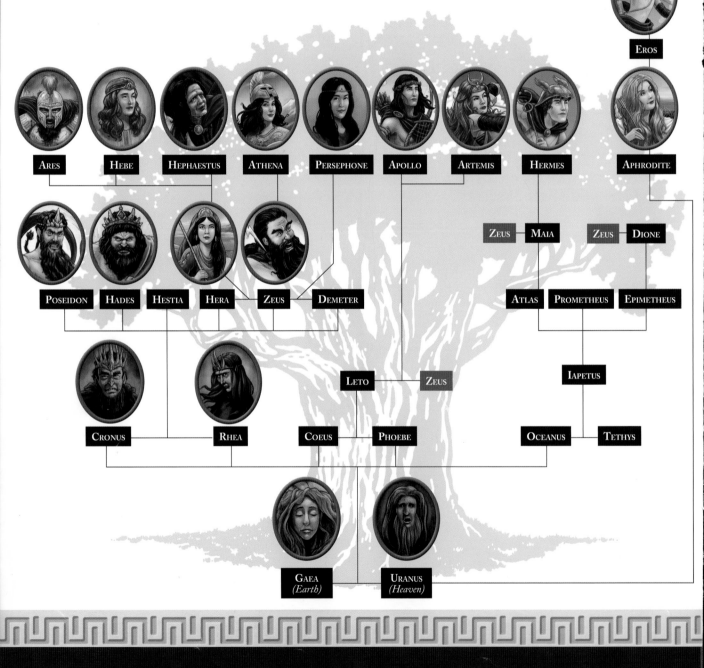

EROS

ARES · HEBE · HEPHAESTUS · ATHENA · PERSEPHONE · APOLLO · ARTEMIS · HERMES · APHRODITE

ZEUS · MAIA · ZEUS · DIONE

POSEIDON · HADES · HESTIA · HERA · ZEUS · DEMETER

ATLAS · PROMETHEUS · EPIMETHEUS

IAPETUS

CRONUS · RHEA · COEUS · PHOEBE · OCEANUS · TETHYS

LETO · ZEUS

GAEA
(Earth) · URANUS
(Heaven)

30

THE ROMAN GODS

s the Roman Empire expanded by conquering new lands the Romans often took on aspects of the customs and beliefs of the people they conquered. From the ancient Greeks they took their arts and sciences. They also adopted many of their gods and the myths that went with them into their religious beliefs. While the names were changed, the stories and legends found a new home.

ZEUS: *Jupiter*
King of the Gods, God of Sky and Storms
Symbols: *Eagle and Thunderbolt*

HERA: *Juno*
Queen of the Gods, Goddess of Marriage
Symbols: *Peacock, Cow, and Crow*

POSEIDON: *Neptune*
God of the Sea and Earthquakes
Symbols: *Trident, Horse, and Dolphin*

HADES: *Pluto*
God of the Underworld
Symbols: *Helmet, Metals, and Jewels*

ATHENA: *Minerva*
Goddess of Wisdom, War, and Crafts
Symbols: *Owl, Shield, and Olive Branch*

ARES: *Mars*
God of War
Symbols: *Vulture and Dog*

ARTEMIS: *Diana*
Goddess of Hunting and Protector of Animals
Symbols: *Stag and Moon*

APOLLO: *Apollo*
God of the Sun, Healing, Music, and Poetry
Symbols: *Laurel, Lyre, Bow, and Raven*

HEPHAESTUS: *Vulcan*
God of Fire, Metalwork, and Building
Symbols: *Fire, Hammer, and Donkey*

APHRODITE: *Venus*
Goddess of Love and Beauty
Symbols: *Dove, Sparrow, Swan, and Myrtle*

EROS: *Cupid*
God of Love
Symbols: *Quiver and Arrows*

HERMES: *Mercury*
God of Travels and Trade
Symbols: *Staff, Winged Sandals, and Helmet*

FURTHER INFORMATION

BOOKS

Green, Jen. *Ancient Greek Myths*. New York: Gareth Stevens, 2010.

Napoli, Donna Jo. *Treasury of Greek Mythology: Classic Stories of Gods, Goddesses, Heroes & Monsters*. Washington, DC: National Geographic Society, 2011.

O'Neal, Claire. *Artemis*. Hockessin, DE: Mitchell Lane, 2008.

WEB SITES

Visit our Web site for links about Artemis: **childsworld.com/links**

Note to Parents, Teachers, and Librarians: We routinely verify our Web links to make sure they are safe and active sites. So encourage your readers to check them out!

INDEX

Actaeon, 18–19
Agamemnon, King, 27
Aloadae giants, 23
ancient Greek society, 5, 28
ancient Greek theater, 18
Apollo, 10, 15, 20, 23
Artemis,
    attendants, 12, 16, 18
    birth, 10
    hunting dogs, 12
    temple, 28
Atalanta, 24
Callisto, 16
Calydon, 24
Calydonian boar, 24

Crete, 20
Cyclopes, 12
Delos, Greece, 10
Echo, 16
Eileithyia, 10
Hera, 8–10, 23
Iphigenia, 27
Jason, 24
Leto, 8–10, 15
Melanion, 24
Meleager, 24
Metamorphoses, 15
Mount Olympus, 8, 10, 23
Mount Sipylus, 15
Mycenae, 27

Narcissus, 16
Niobe, 15
nymphs, 12, 16, 18
Oeneus, King, 24
Orion, 20, 21, 23
Ovid, 14–15
Pan, 12–13
Python, 9
Scorpius constellation, 20–21
storytellers, 5
Tauris, 27
Theseus, 24
Trojan War, 27
Troy, 27
Zeus, 8, 10, 12, 15, 16, 24